ROCKY MOUNTAIN REVENGE

RHONDA STARNES

LOVE INSPIRED SUSPENSE
INSPIRATIONAL ROMANCE

Recycling programs
for this product may
not exist in your area.

ISBN-13: 978-1-335-72184-6

Rocky Mountain Revenge

This edition published by arrangement with Harlequin Books S.A.

For questions and comments about the quality of this book, please contact us at CustomerService@Harlequin.com.

Love Inspired
22 Adelaide St. West, 40th Floor
Toronto, Ontario M5H 4E3, Canada
www.Harlequin.com

Printed in U.S.A.

And be ye kind one to another, tenderhearted, forgiving one another, even as God for Christ's sake hath forgiven you.

—Ephesians 4:32

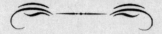

For my husband, Coy, who told me to stop talking about "one day" and either write a book or shut up. You have always been my biggest cheerleader, and I would not have achieved this dream without you. Thank you for being my happily-ever-after.

For my children and grandchildren. You are my greatest blessings. I love you forever!

For my dad, I'm so thankful you and Mom raised me to work hard and never give up. My biggest regret is not chasing this dream sooner, so Mom would have been here to celebrate.

Also, special thanks to:

My editor, Tina James, for making my dream of being a Love Inspired Suspense author come true and for helping me teach my students that hard work pays off.

Connie Queen, for asking me if I wanted to be critique partners six years ago. What a journey it has been. We made it!

Tina Radcliffe, for your guidance and wisdom and for encouraging me when I grew weary.

My writing sisters and critique partners, for your encouragement, support and prayers.

My family, friends and students for cheering me on.

ONE

Grace Porter regretted she hadn't stopped for fuel before leaving Denver two hours ago, when it was still daylight. If she had, she wouldn't be at a run-down gas station that looked like it belonged in a low-budget horror movie. A dim yellow light flickered overhead and made a strange buzzing sound. The attendant, a tall, gaunt man with oily brown hair, stood behind the counter and stared at her through the window, reminding her of Norman Bates.

At least the two pumps had been updated to the pay-at-the-pump variety, so she wouldn't have to go inside.

She pulled the nozzle out of the car's gas tank, settled it back on its cradle and drummed her fingers on the side of her red Honda CRV as she waited for the receipt to print. Though she wasn't typically scared of shadows in the dark, the overcast night sky obscured the moon and stars, providing little visibility outside the immediate rim of the artificial light from the gas station awning. A light breeze made the already cool late-May night air even colder, sending a shiver up her arms.

Why was she feeling uneasy? She'd filled up her car at this very station numerous times when she was younger, often late at night when heading home from a friend's house. Had living in Denver the past eight years made her dependent on streetlights on every corner for a sense of security?

Hopefully, she would only be in Blackberry Falls for a couple of months then she could return to her life in Denver. In the meantime, she would provide emotional support to her sister, Chloe, as she finalized her divorce. She would also have to focus on hiring someone to replace James, her soon-to-be ex-brother-in-law, as the veterinarian at the animal clinic she and Chloe had inherited two years ago.

Grace had never wanted to be a small-town veterinarian, but here she was about to temporarily take over the reins of the clinic her father had built. Something he'd always wanted but she'd always tried to avoid.

Chloe couldn't be expected to continue working with James until a replacement could be found. It had been difficult enough for her sister to continue going to work as the clinic's office manager the past few months while Grace worked out the details of her leave of absence from the animal hospital in Denver where she worked as a veterinary cardiologist.

Grace didn't understand her sister's emotional attachment to their hometown and would have suggested Chloe walk away and start fresh in a new city if she thought her words would have been welcomed.

She startled at the sudden blare of music emanating from her vehicle. Chloe's ringtone. Grace tore off the receipt, shoved it into the back pocket of her jeans and slid behind the steering wheel. Grabbing her phone off the dashboard, she slid a finger across the screen, silencing Sister Sledge in the middle of "We Are Family." Her sister's face filled the screen.

"Chloe. Why are you FaceTiming? What if I were driving?"

Chloe's blue eyes sparkled. "I checked the app and saw that you had stopped for gas."

"Then you also saw I'm only ten minutes away." Grace smiled.

"I know, but I got held up at the clinic and just arrived home."

Chloe had always hated going into an empty house by herself after dark. When she couldn't avoid doing that, she would call Grace to video chat as she entered the house, claiming it made her feel less alone. Her theory was that Grace could call 9-1-1 if there was an intruder.

This was getting out of hand. Maybe, while Grace was back in Blackberry Falls, she could finally get Chloe to install an alarm system and sign up for self-defense classes.

Grace sighed. "Okay. But be fast."

Chloe exited her vehicle. "Man, it's dark out here tonight. Good thing you gave me this flashlight key chain for Christmas last year. It's the only reason I haven't tripped and busted my face."

Her sister never would have stayed out late on such a dark night if she could have helped it. "What kept you at the clinic so late?"

"We can discuss that after you get here. Oh, but I do need to tell you, I received another letter from Benjamin Hamilton wanting to purchase the farm."

The farm was eighty acres of prime pastureland and the two-story farmhouse they had lived in growing up. It had sat empty since their father died, until Chloe moved back in several months ago. Grace had no need of the property and planned to sign over her share to Chloe once her divorce was finalized.

"Didn't you tell him you plan to live there permanently?"

"I did. His recent letter lists all the reasons

I shouldn't live out here alone." Keys jingled. "Hang on a second while I open the door."

The screen went black. "Chloe, I can't see you. The screen says 'Poor Connection.'"

A thud boomed across the line, and her sister's scream split the air. "No! No-o-o!"

Grace's heart pounded. The video reconnected, but the ceiling had replaced her sister's image.

"Chloe. Are you okay? What's happening?" Grace yelled into the phone.

Had Chloe's Great Dane, Barkley, knocked her down?

"Chloe! Answer me. Right now."

The sound of a struggle and furniture being knocked over echoed in the background. "Okay, I'm calling nine-one-one."

A person wearing a full-face novelty ski mask that resembled a black bear stared into the phone. Brown eyes glared at her, assessing.

An involuntary gasp escaped Grace's lips as she covered her mouth with a trembling hand.

"Go ahead. It'll be too late by the time they get here." He laughed and the screen went blank.

Pressing the call button on the steering wheel, she put the vehicle into gear and sped out of the parking lot.

"Nine-one-one. What's your emergency?"

"My sister." Grace took the curve at New-

found Gap fast. Too fast. Except right now
there was no such thing as too fast. "Chloe Osborne, 1362 Monteagle Lane. Someone broke
in. I heard a struggle and a scream. There's a
masked man, and the phone went blank."

"There's an intruder?"

Wasn't that what she'd said? Grace bit back
angry words and fought to stay calm. "Yes—
1362 Monteagle Lane."

The dispatcher repeated the address. Then,
"What is your name?"

What did that matter? Why weren't they
sending a troop of police cars, lights flashing
and sirens screaming, to Chloe's house?

*The nearest neighbors are a half mile away.
There's no one to hear my sister's cries for help.*

"Ma'am, your name?"

"Grace. Dr. Grace Porter. Chloe's my sister.
Why aren't you sending help?"

"Help is on the way."

The dispatcher's calm voice infuriated Grace.
Chloe's life was in danger! How could she be
so absolutely nonchalant?

*She's supposed to be calm. That's why she's
got this job. Breathe. Think. Pray.*

But she couldn't breathe. Not normally. Or
think. The only thing she could envision was
Chloe's worst nightmare coming true. Being

on the phone with Grace hadn't stopped it from happening.

Disconnecting the call, she pressed harder on the accelerator.

Please, Lord, let help arrive in time.

She turned onto the road that led to her childhood home and pulled up to the edge of the property, cutting the engine. Even from this distance, she could see the front door was open. Lights spilled out from the downstairs windows.

Now what? There was no sign of the police yet.

She couldn't sit there. Her sister might be injured. Or worse—dead.

What could she use as a weapon?

Digging through the glove compartment, she found a flashlight, an ice scraper and the vehicle owner's manual.

Ugh, what else do I have?

She felt under the passenger seat. An umbrella. Success!

Thankful for the cover of darkness, she sprinted across the lawn. Reaching the corner of the two-story farmhouse, she inched along the side, stopping at every window to peek and listen.

A whimpering growl sounded. She pressed her face against the cool glass of the window. Barkley, locked in a bedroom, clawed at the door. Desperate to save his owner. Grace's veterinarian heart bled for him, but she couldn't offer comforting words for fear he'd reveal her presence.

She reached the porch and climbed. One. Step. At. A. Time.

Muffled voices reached her. Chloe's and a man's. Deep and guttural.

Umbrella at the ready, she entered the house and stopped short. Chloe, her back to the stairs, was struggling with her attacker on the second-floor landing.

The faint sound of a siren pierced the night. *Thank you, Lord.*

The masked man met her eyes above Chloe's head, and for a split second, she wondered if she'd spoken the words out loud.

Inching closer to the stairs, Grace battled the desire to race up to them. If she distracted her sister from her mission of survival, it could be catastrophic. Chloe must have sensed her presence because she glanced over her shoulder. That was all the edge the attacker needed.

He pushed Chloe, and her body bent backward over the railing. She had one hand gripping the wood rail, the other grasping his mask.

Grace charged. Before she made it even midway up the curved staircase, her sister flew through the air.

"Chloe!"

She landed on the foyer floor in a heap, a ski mask in her outstretched hand.

Grace rushed down. Footsteps pounded on the stairs right behind her. She looked over her shoulder. A man in his midforties, with collar-length brown hair and a scruffy beard sprinkled with gray, smirked at her.

She raised the umbrella to ward off an attack. The man ducked and head-butted her in the side, sending her tumbling down the last four steps.

Pushing herself up onto her hands and knees, she pressed a hand against the wall, struggling to stand.

The man snickered as he planted his booted foot on her back and pushed her flat to the floor. "You're next, Amazing Grace."

She froze. *Amazing Grace. She hadn't heard that name in two years, not since her father died. How did he know Dad's nickname for her?*

Sirens grew louder as red-and-blue strobe lights bounced across the walls. The man sprinted out of sight. Seconds later, she heard the kitchen door, leading into the backyard, bang closed.

Grasping the newel post, she pulled herself to her feet and raced to Chloe, who lay crumpled on her side like a discarded rag doll. A pool of blood seeped out from under her head.

Chloe's breathing was shallow. Grace bent and checked for a pulse. Weak. Placing her hands on either side of Chloe's neck, she pressed in gently with her fingers and ran them up the length of the neck to the base of the head. It did not appear to be broken. Carefully, tilting her sister's head, Grace examined the wound. A bump had already appeared, in the center of which was a gash about two inches long. It didn't seem very deep, but would require stitches.

Grabbing a chunky, knit cardigan off the hook near the door, she knelt beside her sister and applied pressure to the wound. "Hang in there, sis. Help is on the way."

Childhood memories swarmed her as Dad's constant reminder echoed in her mind. *Amazing Grace, as the big sister, it's your job to take care of Chloe.*

Footsteps sounded on the porch. An officer entered the house, gun at the ready. "Are there more intruders?"

Her head snapped in his direction. Hazel eyes pierced hers. Grace's breath caught. She hadn't expected *him* to respond.

"Grace. How many intruders?" Chief Evan Bradshaw's question came out harsher than he intended, but he needed to assess the situation and was barely holding himself back from rushing to her side.

She shook her head. "Only one. He went out the back."

"We saw him. Johnson took off after him." Evan holstered his weapon. "How badly is she hurt?"

"Head wound. Her pulse is weak. Possible internal injuries. Won't know for sure until she has some scans." Grace's voice cracked, and he knew she was struggling to keep her composure.

"Where's the ambulance?" Desperation echoed in her voice. Blue eyes pleaded with him, tears pooling.

Evan clenched his hands at his sides, fighting the urge to pull her into a hug, the way he would have when they were younger.

Instead, he knelt beside her, taking a quick assessment. Grace held a cloth of some sort against Chloe's head. There was a lot of blood, but he knew that wasn't uncommon for head wounds. "She'll be okay, Gracie. I promise."

Now, why had he said that? Who was he to make promises? He'd learned a long time ago he couldn't stop death. Losing his unborn daughter and his wife three months apart had taught him that.

Chloe's pale face stood out in stark contrast

against the bloodstained rug. He watched for the rise and fall of her chest, as he had his now six-year-old son, Camden, when he was an infant. Chloe's breathing was almost imperceptible, but it was steady.

"What's taking the ambulance so long?" Grace wiped her face, silent tears flowing freely now. "I can't lose her."

From the moment they'd met in sixth grade until high school graduation, Evan and Grace had been inseparable. During that time, he had only seen her cry twice. The first time in seventh grade when her cat, Mitzi, died. The second, the summer before their sophomore year of high school when her mom died from cancer. Her crying now meant she'd started to lose hope that Chloe would survive.

He needed to keep Grace busy so her mind didn't wander down the what-if trail. "Go find a blanket. We need to keep her warm until the ambulance arrives."

Her eyes widened. "Shock. Why didn't I think of that?" Tilting Chloe's head so the floor would hold the cloth in place, she crossed the foyer into the living room.

While she did as he asked, Evan used his phone to snap a few photos of Chloe's position. Two of his officers were en route. They'd take additional shots of the perimeter and interior of the house.

Grace returned with a fuzzy, paisley-print throw. She draped it across her sister's body then ran her bloodstained hands along the length of Chloe's arms and legs. "Nothing appears to be broken, but we won't know for sure until she has X-rays."

"Can you tell me what happened?"

"We were on video chat." Her voice shook.

She closed her eyes and took a deep breath. Then her lips moved in silent prayer, something he hadn't done in a long time. He guessed it was some comfort that she could cling to her faith when in distress.

"Take your time."

She met his eyes; her gaze steady, tears gone. "He told me calling nine-one-one wouldn't do any good. Help would arrive too late."

"Who told you?"

"The man who did this. Before he disconnected the call."

Evan's gut tightened. The attacker had seen Grace. He wished he could spare her the questions but knew he couldn't. "Did you see his face?"

"Not then…but when he pushed Chloe over the banister, she pulled off his ski mask." Grace nodded to the black fabric in Chloe's out-stretched hand.

How had he missed seeing this important piece of evidence?

Get your head into the game, Bradshaw. Don't let Grace's presence throw you. You're not a lovesick teen any longer.

Turning back to her, he asked, "Did you recognize the attacker?"

"No."

She shivered, and once again, he clenched his hands. Why did he think he had to touch her to comfort her? He'd always strove to be compassionate to victims and witnesses, but he'd never wanted to embrace one before. The way he did her. Could the instinct simply be a muscle memory?

"He knew me." Her whisper was barely audible.

Evan's gut tightened. "What did you say?"

"Chloe's attacker knew me. He called me Amazing Grace."

Dr. Porter had been the only one to call his daughter Amazing Grace. Even Evan had never called her by that nickname, respecting the bond she had with her dad.

"He said I was next," she whispered.

Evan bit back an exclamation. He couldn't allow her to see that her words had shaken him.

The dying wail of a siren announced the arrival of the ambulance.

A dog howled from somewhere deep within the house.

"Barkley," Grace said. "I forgot all about him. He's locked in the master bedroom."

Two EMTs entered the house wearing trauma–jump bag backpacks. Evan gave a silent signal to let them know they could take care of the victim but couldn't move anything.

Lieutenant Johnson entered the house right behind the medics. He met Evan's eyes and gave a slight shake of his head. Suspect not apprehended.

Pulling Grace away from Chloe, Evan whispered, "Give them room to work." He turned her to face him and jerked his head toward the hall. The sound of Chloe's dog's whimpering grew louder. "Why don't you go check on Barkley?"

"But…" She looked from him to Chloe and back again, the internal struggle etched on her face.

"Go. You're the vet. Make sure Barkley is okay." He smiled. Encouraging her to trust him. "I'll stay here. Chloe won't leave my sight."

The medics spoke in low tones behind them. Checking vitals. Making decisions.

Grace nodded, a wisp of blond hair falling in her face. His hand froze in midair. Another muscle memory. He let his hand drop to his side. He didn't have the right to brush hair out of her face. And hadn't in fifteen years, not since the day of high school graduation when she'd decided Evan and Blackberry Falls weren't enough for her. "Go on. I'll let you know when they're ready to transport her."

Grace wiped away a tear, offered him a shaky smile of thanks and then turned and went down the hall.

As soon as she was out of range, he snapped more photos with his cell phone and bagged the ski mask. Rage reverberated through him when he saw the image screen-printed on the fleece mask. Being attacked was brutal. Being attacked by someone looking like a black bear seemed extra cruel.

He nodded to the stocky, bald medic. Patterson, according to his name badge. "How bad is she?"

"Critical."

"Please, save her."

"That's always our goal, man." Patterson inclined his head toward the outdoors. "How well do you know this area? I need a place for my medical transport pilot to land."

"There's a hay field, past the barn, about a hundred and fifty feet behind the house."

"That'll work."

"Two officers are arriving on scene now. I'll have them park where their headlights illuminate the area."

Evan radioed his officers as the EMTs worked to stabilize Chloe. Then he pulled Johnson aside.

"Where'd the guy go?"

"I'm not sure, boss. I chased him through the woods and across the creek that borders the Hamilton Thoroughbred Ranch before I lost him. He took off in an old black truck."

"I can't imagine the Hamiltons allowing just anyone to park on their property. You think he works for them?"

"I don't know, but he knew the terrain, giving him an advantage over me."

"Did you go up to the main house and talk to Ben?"

"I did. It took several minutes to get someone to the door. Ben said he and Mrs. Hamilton were watching a movie in the basement, so he hadn't heard any vehicles leaving the property."

"Surely you described the truck to him. Did he have any idea who it could belong to?"

His lieutenant shook his head. "He said, and I quote, 'If I spent all my time trying to keep track of my employees' vehicles, I wouldn't have time to run my ranch.'"

Evan bit back a retort as Grace walked toward him. A massive fawn-colored Great Dane trailed behind her, the top of his head almost reaching her shoulder. The animal easily outweighed her by seventy pounds or more. It was a sight to behold.

"This must be Barkley," Evan said.

The medic who was kneeling beside Chloe moved, and before anyone could stop the dog, he walked over to his mistress and put his nose to her chest. Grace whistled, and the animal ambled back to her side.

"I couldn't keep him contained any longer. He needed to see her." She shrugged. "So did I."

"It's okay," Evan replied. "I was about to come get you. They're getting ready to transport her to Denver Memorial."

"Denver? That's over two hours away." She didn't take her eyes off the medical team as they secured Chloe to a stretcher, an IV already pushing vital fluids through her veins. "Wouldn't County be closer?"

"Denver Memorial is one of the best trauma hospitals in the state." The house rumbled as the air ambulance helicopter flew overhead.

"I want to go with her. Make them take me with her." She clutched his arm, her voice pleading.

Evan shook his head. His chest tightened at the pain in her eyes. "Gracie, they don't have enough room to take passengers. Besides, we've got to take care of Barkley before we leave."

"But…"

"I'll get you to Denver. Fast. You'll be the first person to see her after the doctors have run all their tests."

"What if *he* gets to her first?" Her shoulders slumped.

Unable to resist, he pulled her into a tight embrace. He would regret it later. But she was hurting, and for now, he was the only one she had to lean on. "He won't. I promise."

"How can you promise that?" She spoke into his chest. "Denver is outside your jurisdiction."

Evan pulled back and looked down at her. He didn't care what it took. Even if he had to pay for a private security guard himself, he would not let her down. "I promise. She will have a guard twenty-four seven until her attacker has been caught." *And so will you.*

TWO

Grace stepped out of Evan's arms, avoiding eye contact. Her cheeks warmed. Why had he pulled her into an embrace? More importantly, why had she allowed him to? Because she had been worried about Chloe. No other reason. He had only been offering comfort in a time of distress. A perfectly normal reaction. Almost half of her life had been lived since walking away from him the day he proposed. She had moved on. So had he.

After she moved to Fort Collins for college and then settled in Denver, Chloe and Dad had made it their mission in life to keep her up-to-date on current events in Blackberry Falls, including Evan getting married, becoming a father and then losing his wife.

The embrace had simply been an old friend offering comfort. Nothing more.

"Logroll to the left on three. One...two... three."

The commanding voice penetrated Grace's foggy brain and the activity around her came into focus.

"Okay, guys, let's move."

"No. Wait!" She pushed past Evan and chased after the medics carrying Chloe out of the house. Racing down the steps of the porch, she touched the arm of the medic at the head of the backboard. "One minute. Please."

He nodded. "One minute."

Grace brushed Chloe's light brown hair out of her face. She longed to see her sister's laughing, blue eyes, but they remained closed. "I'll be at the hospital as soon as I get Barkley taken care of. I love you, sis." She gently kissed Chloe's forehead and stepped back. *Please, Lord, let her be okay.*

The medics continued toward the helicopter. She jogged alongside them until a strong hand pulled her back at the edge of the field.

Turning, she met Evan's eyes. No point asking if she could drive herself to the hospital. She had enough sense to know she shouldn't travel alone, not after she'd seen the attacker's face. "How soon can we leave?"

"I need to give Johnson a few instructions." He nodded at the Great Dane at her side. "What are you going to do with him?"

"We'll take him to the clinic. If there's no

room in the kennel, I'll leave him in the apartment upstairs. If I'm not back by morning, I can have one of the staff feed and walk him." She sighed. "As a matter of fact, I probably need to take my car and leave my stuff there. Then I won't have to come back here."

A look flashed in his eyes, as if he might argue, but he didn't. "Get whatever Barkley needs. I'll be ready when you're finished."

"Five minutes. That's all I need." She ran her hand over the dog's back. "Come on, boy."

True to his word, Evan was ready to go as soon as she returned. She quickly loaded Barkley into the backseat of her Honda CRV and pulled out of the drive. Evan followed behind in his gray department-issued SUV with the Blackberry Falls PD logo emblazoned on the side.

Ten minutes later, she pulled into the employee parking area at the side of Porter Animal Clinic, an old stone-and-cedar building on the edge of town. The structure had evolved over the nearly forty years of its existence, expanding to more than three times its original size. The sight of the business her father built through hard work and dedication brought a flood of emotions. She thought of Dad every single day. Had it only been two years since that automobile accident had taken his life? Seemed much longer. Grief compressed her heart, squeezing her chest. Would she lose Chloe, too?

Grace had barely put the vehicle into Park when Evan tapped on her window. "Don't cut the engine."

"What? Why?"

"I need to check the area to make sure no one is lurking around or waiting inside." He slipped his gun out of its holster. "I want you outta here fast if something happens."

Grace's mouth went dry. Her throat tightened, making it impossible to get words out. She hadn't even thought about the possibility the attacker could be waiting for her here.

"It'll be okay. Keep your doors locked and the engine running. If I'm not back in ten minutes, get out of here. Go straight to the station. Got it?"

She nodded agreement.

Thankful Chloe had always insisted she have easy access to the clinic they co-owned even if she didn't work there, Grace handed him keys and wrote down the pass codes to the security system and the lock on the apartment door. Then she rolled up her window and watched as he entered the darkened building.

What on earth had she come home to? Her breath caught and tears stung her eyes. *Lord, please let Chloe be okay. Don't let me lose my sister like this.*

She took some steadying breaths. It wouldn't help Chloe for her to fall apart. The only thing she could do for her sister at this moment was to help figure out the identity of their attacker. Why had he attacked Chloe in the first place? She was fairly certain the guy hadn't been a robber caught off guard when the homeowner returned. If he had been, why had he threatened Grace? Even calling her by her childhood nickname. She'd been distracted enough when Chloe had fallen. He could have taken the back stairs down to the kitchen and escaped without her seeing his face.

To her knowledge, her sister didn't have any enemies. Was this connected to the clinic? If it was, why had the man said she was next in a way that made it seem like that had always been his plan and wasn't just because she'd seen his face? Other than being a silent partner, Grace had nothing to do with the clinic.

Did this have something to do with Chloe and James's divorce? Grace had a hard time believing James would want to harm Chloe. He'd always seemed so devoted to her...but apparently things were not always as they seemed on the surface. He'd put her sister through so much anguish.

Should she call him to tell him about the attack? Legally, he was Chloe's husband, at least for another week until the divorce was finalized. Maybe Evan could advise her about contacting him.

A shiver racked her body. She rubbed her arms and took concentrated breaths. Needing to do something constructive, she dug into her purse and pulled out a pen and an old receipt. She flipped the receipt over and jotted down details about the attacker as they flashed in her mind.

Midforties. Brown eyes. Dark brown hair—collar-length, wavy, some graying. Oblong face. Cleft chin.

Height? Hmm. This one was harder. The man had been standing at the top of the stairs. Though, he hadn't seemed much more than half a foot taller than Chloe's five-four frame.

To the list, she added "five-ten" followed by a question mark.

Grace tapped the pen on the steering wheel and glanced at the dashboard. Eleven thirty-seven. Evan had been inside nine minutes. Where was he? She peered through the windshield. The clinic had never seemed scary before, but tonight she noticed the shadowed areas around the building. She'd have additional lighting installed the first chance she got.

Dogs barked in the kennel that connected to the back of the building and ran parallel to the parking area. Someone moved along the perimeter inside the fence. Her breath caught, then she exhaled. Evan. She'd recognize his confident stride anywhere.

Evan was a good man, hardworking and loyal. She wasn't surprised when he'd been promoted to chief of police at the young age of thirty, the youngest in Blackberry Falls' history. He had always been a planner; when he set goals, he reached them.

When he'd proposed to her the night they'd graduated high school, he'd had their whole life planned. They would attend Colorado State University Pueblo, each taking a hefty course load to complete their bachelor degrees in three years. After graduation, Evan would attend the police academy and Grace would transfer to Colorado State University in Fort Collins to complete her Doctor of Veterinary Medicine PhD, which would have meant a long-distance relationship for four years. They'd marry after she graduated and settle in Blackberry Falls. Though she'd loved him deeply and had dreamed of a life with him, it had all seemed a bit too much to her eighteen-year-old self. She'd bolted.

Would things have been different if she had

agreed to return to Blackberry Falls and marry him? One thing was for sure, if she had returned home, Dad wouldn't have hired James and Chloe wouldn't have gone through the heartache and disappointment he'd put her through the past few years.

What else would have been different? Would Chloe still have been attacked tonight? Would Grace be afraid for her life?

Evan slipped back into the clinic and closed the door, muffling the sound of the barking. He'd cleared the interior and exterior. No signs of an intruder, at least not one still hanging around. There were a couple of areas of concern, namely an unlocked exterior door and an office behind the reception area that looked like it may have been ransacked. Either that or the person who the office belonged to was a bit of a slob.

He flipped on the hall light and headed for the side entrance to get Grace and Chloe's miniature-horse-size dog. They needed to get the Great Dane settled quickly and be on their way to the hospital.

His cell phone vibrated with a text message from his former high school football teammate. Ryan Vincent was a co-owner of the private security firm Protective Instincts. Evan had called him on the drive to the clinic and requested his assistance.

At hospital. I'm stationed outside Chloe's ER room. Bridget is in waiting area on lookout. See you when you get here.

Evan wasn't sure how Ryan had received permission to enter the examination area of the ER, but he was thankful to have a friend with those kinds of connections.

He typed a quick reply.

10-4. Thanks. ETA 2 hours.

If I exceed the speed limit and don't run into any trouble.

For Grace's sake, he needed to make the trip as quickly as possible. Or was it for his sake? The ride could get awkward. They hadn't spent more than a few minutes in each other's presence since the day of high school graduation. Not that he had any lingering feelings for her. He had grown up and realized a childhood love rarely manifested into a lifelong, lasting relationship. He'd moved on, discovering Grace had made the right decision by not marrying him. If Evan had learned one thing from his marriage, it was that he wasn't marriage material. Now a widower and single father of a six-year-old boy, he'd likely remain single.

Camden. His son was a blessing. Thankfully, he was spending the night with his maternal grandparents.

Evan exited the building and found Grace standing at the back of her SUV, Barkley at her side. The cargo liftgate was open.

"What are you doing out of the vehicle?" He increased his stride and reached her side in time to lift the large suitcase out of the back.

"I'm unloading the necessities." She shrugged. "I saw the light come on, so I figured all was safe."

He scrubbed his hand across his face. "Still. You should have waited on me."

"I knew you were on your way out, and we're in a hurry. We need to get to the hospital ASAP."

He couldn't argue with that, but he'd have to find a way to make her understand the seriousness of the situation. She was a target.

Evan sighed. In a few minutes, they were going to be inside a vehicle for a two-hour drive. He'd wait until then to hammer home the facts and how she had to follow his instructions if she wanted to stay safe.

"Get the dog. I've got the bag." He closed the liftgate and ushered her into the building. "As far as I could tell, both the indoor and outdoor kennels looked full."

Animals barked and meowed in the far reaches of the clinic, masking their footsteps on the old tile floors. If he hadn't already cleared the building, he'd be concerned someone could sneak up on them in this environment.

"That's okay. It's probably best to leave Barkley in the apartment. It'll feel more like home." Grace started up the stairs, and he touched her arm and halted her.

"About that. The exterior door to the apartment was unlocked when I went in. Maybe no one thought physically locking it was important since there's a digital door lock. But that's not the case. While it's convenient not having to dig out a key, digital locks are easily hacked."

Surprise registered on her face, and her eyes widened. "It should have been locked. We always use both the key and the code to enter the exterior door."

"The apartment looked undisturbed. I'll need you to do a quick check, though, to be sure nothing is missing."

They entered the small one-bedroom apartment, and Grace did a hurried walk-through. "Nothing seems to be missing, but I can't be positive. It's been almost two years since I last stayed here."

That would mean she hadn't been home since Andrew Porter had died. Though he'd rarely run into Grace when she'd come to Blackberry Falls, it surprised him it had been so long since she'd visited. Maybe coming home after losing her dad had been too painful.

Evan probably understood the pain of loss better than anyone. It had been difficult for him to return home after his wife had been murdered. Beautiful, compassionate Lisa. He'd felt the loss of her presence everywhere in town. Eventually, he learned to avoid the painful places. Even finding excuses not to attend church, where he missed her sweet, soprano voice and the feel of her hand in his during prayer in the early years of their marriage. Before she'd slipped into depression.

He'd let Lisa down as a husband and as a protector. Most days, he barely stayed a step ahead of the wave of guilt that threatened to drown him.

There would be no way to outrun the tsunami that would engulf him if he failed to protect Gracie, too.

Grace filled Barkley's water bowl and placed it a few feet from his dog bed. "All done. Let's get to the hospital."

It had been an hour since the air ambulance

had transported Chloe to Memorial, and Grace was anxious to get to the ER to see if her sister was awake. She also wanted to question the doctor about Chloe's condition.

Evan motioned for her to lead the way down the stairs and back through the clinic. "I need you to check one more room before we leave."

She half turned on the stairs to look at him, raising an eyebrow. What had he found on his walk-through?

"The office tucked in the corner behind the receptionist desk looks like it may have been ransacked. Or the person it belongs to is unorganized and messy."

Grace pressed her lips together to suppress the laughter bubbling up inside her.

"What's so funny?" Evan looked at her like she'd lost her mind.

Nothing. Nothing at all. Sadness washed over her. Chloe's messiness had been a family joke for years.

She took a few steadying breaths. "That's Chloe's office. Unorganized and messy is her nature. I'll look, but I can almost guarantee the mess has Chloe written all over it."

He led her to her sister's office, stopping her in the doorway. "Don't touch anything until you're sure it's the way Chloe would have left it."

She nodded. "Sure. No prob—"

The front door of the clinic burst open, and Evan pushed her into the office, turning to block her as he pulled his gun.

"What is going on?" James Osborne's voice boomed. "Why are you prowling around my clinic, chief?"

"First, it's not *your* clinic. Second, I'm not prowling."

"Oh, really. Then why did several of the neighbors call to tell me someone was skulking through the kennels, upsetting the dogs?"

Grace tamped down the anger that threatened. The busybodies of Blackberry Falls were at it again. If any of those neighbors had looked closely, they would have seen it was the police chief's SUV in the parking lot and not an intruder's. Or maybe they had noticed and were looking to start the gossip mill. She sighed and slipped further out of sight. At least she no longer had to figure out whether or not to notify James about the night's events.

Evan holstered his weapon and walked into the reception area, his footsteps echoing on the tile floor.

"There was an incident at the farm this evening. Grace and I thought it best to bring Barkley here."

"What? Where's Chloe?"

Thankful Evan was the one dealing with

James, she turned and looked at her sister's office, tuning out the conversation in the reception area.

A raincoat, two Porter Animal Clinic T-shirts and an oversize tote bag covered the filing cabinet in the corner. It looked more like forgotten exercise equipment in someone's bedroom than an important piece of office furniture. In typical Chloe fashion, files that should have been in the cabinet were stacked in multiple piles on the desk. Even with modern technology, her sister preferred to work with paper copies. Once accounts were settled, she knew Chloe scanned copies into the computer and shredded the originals. A few files she'd obviously been working on before leaving work for the day lay open, contents scattered across her closed laptop. Could the laptop hold answers to Chloe's attack?

When Chloe had called to tell her about her marriage problems, she'd also mentioned that some things at the clinic hadn't been adding up lately. Hence, Grace taking a leave of absence and returning home to take over the clinic from James while they searched for a replacement.

The men's footsteps drew closer. Grabbing the tote bag off the cabinet, she quickly shoved the folders and the laptop into it. Then she noticed a file without a label peeking out from under the desk blotter. She shoved it into the bag, slipped the strap over her shoulder and turned, making eye contact with Evan as he and James entered the room. He glanced at the tote and raised an eyebrow. She prayed he wouldn't ask about the bag and James would think it was just her oversize purse.

"Grace!" James pushed past Evan and came to stand in front of her. Gray eyes looked at her accusingly. "Why didn't you call to tell me someone attacked Chloe and she was injured?"

She took a deep breath, releasing it before answering. "I wasn't sure of proper protocol since she's your ex-wife...or she will be after next week."

"I realize that." He shoved a hand through his short, chestnut-colored hair. "It doesn't mean I don't want to know what's happening to her."

"I'm sorry. I had planned to call you once we left here. Chloe and Barkley had to be my primary focus."

"Of course. You're right. The main thing is I know now. So, come on. I'll drive you to the hospital, and we'll find out how she is." He grasped her wrist and dragged her toward the door.

Grace pulled free, stepping back and bumping against the desk. She rubbed her wrist.

James turned and took a step in her direction.

"Whoa." Evan blocked his path. "As Grace pointed out, you're in the middle of a divorce. There's no reason for you to go to the hospital. I'll take her as planned."

"But—"

"No, James." She offered a sympathetic smile. After all he'd put her sister through, Grace never would have thought she'd ever feel sorry for James. "Evan's right. I know you don't automatically stop caring about someone because the relationship is over. But you no longer have the right to be by their side when they're injured or in pain."

For the second time in as many hours, she avoided Evan's eyes, remembering how she'd had to restrain herself from driving down to check on him a few times in the past fifteen years—most recently, four years ago when she'd heard of his wife's murder. He'd been her childhood best friend, and a part of her would always want to know he was okay. But, like James, that hadn't given her the right to be where she wasn't needed. Or wanted.

She touched his arm. "I'll let you know how she is. I promise."

"Okay. I'll be at home, waiting for your call."

"Actually," Evan interjected, "I'd like you to stop by the station first."

"What? Why?"

"I need you to give a statement."

James paled. "You can't think I was the one who attacked Chloe."

"No. I sa—" Grace swallowed the rest of her words when Evan squeezed her hand and gave a subtle shake of his head.

"I'm an upstanding member of this community." Anger flashed in James's eyes as his voice rose. "Just because my wife decided she didn't want to be married any longer doesn't mean I'd want to kill her."

His words struck her like a sharp jab to the solar plexus. Chloe had told her about James's temper, but she'd never seen a hint of it before now. He had always been soft-spoken and mild-mannered.

"Look. I'm not accusing you of anything. It's standard practice to interview the husband, especially if the parties are in the middle of a divorce." Evan's tone softened like he was talking to a buddy. "Honestly, I fully expect your alibi to check out. What I'm really hoping is that you can offer some insight into who might be behind the attack."

James's jaw twitched. After a long pause, he conceded. "Okay."

They all exited the building and locked up. As they turned to leave, Evan clapped James on the back. "I'll call Lieutenant Johnson and let him know to expect you."

James opened his mouth, then closed it. He looked as if he still wanted to argue, but he nodded, climbed into his vehicle and sped away.

Evan opened the door for Grace. She settled into the passenger seat of the police SUV, thankful there was room for her up front so she didn't have to ride in the backseat like a prisoner. Then he jogged around the front of the vehicle, slid behind the steering wheel, started the engine and backed out of the parking lot.

"Okay Gracie, now that we're alone, why don't you tell me what's in the bag besides the file I saw you swipe?"

THREE

"I'll answer all of your questions," Grace said. "After I call the hospital to check on Chloe."

"Do you think they'll tell you anything over the phone?"

It was just like him to express aloud the concerns she was trying desperately to silence in her head. "I don't know. But I've gotta try."

He gave a slight nod. She performed a quick internet search on her phone and located the number. How had anyone survived not knowing the well-being of loved ones in pre–cell phone days?

After fifteen minutes of being transferred multiple times and finally getting to talk to someone in the ER, she disconnected. "All they could tell me was that she is stable and the doctor will talk to me once I get to the hospital."

"Stable is good, right?"

"I don't know. It may be their standard reply

to anyone who calls to ask about a patient." She bit her lower lip.

"I'm sure she's receiving the best care."

"I know. But what if her attacker gets to her before we can?" Grace shifted in her seat, the vinyl squeaking in protest.

He activated the blinker and took the access ramp onto an almost empty interstate. "I already have a guard outside her door."

"Who? How did you get someone there so fast?" She studied his profile. While some men his age were graying, his copper-colored hair had developed blond highlights, which made him look younger than his thirty-three years.

"Do you remember Ryan Vincent?"

"Played football with you, right? Was two or three years behind us in school? His parents own the Flying V Ranch." She paused, picturing the family that hosted church fellowship picnics on their ranch every summer on the Fourth of July. "He had four brothers and one sister... I don't remember her name...but she and Chloe were good friends in school."

"Yeah. Well, Ryan is now co-owner of the private security agency Protective Instincts, based in Denver. On the drive to the clinic, I called to see if he had a bodyguard he could send to the hospital until we got there."

Relief washed over her. "I'm so glad he could send someone."

"Actually, Ryan is the guard outside Chloe's room. His sister—Bridget—is at the hospital, too. On lookout in the waiting room."

"Really? Wow. Send me their bill when you receive it. I'm more than happy to pay whatever it costs."

He shook his head, a frown marring his face. "You don't get it, do you?" Sadness laced his words. "Ryan and Bridget are helping a friend from home. They aren't going to send a bill requesting payment for the time they're at the hospital tonight."

"But protecting people is their business. Not paying them would be like going to a doctor who's an acquaintance and expecting a free examination."

"No. It's like being at the park and twisting your ankle. The town doctor who has known you your entire life is there. He wraps your ankle and instructs you to ice it when you get home. He will not send you a bill, unless you go to him for follow-up treatments. Then he'll bill you for his services." Evan spared her a quick glance before turning his attention back to the road. "If we need to hire Protective Instincts to provide around-the-clock protection for Chloe—which is likely, unless I can get the

Denver PD to provide a guard—then we'll figure out how they need to bill their services."

Grace opened her mouth and closed it again. Evan would think she had lost her mind if she mentioned she'd rather hire someone who wasn't from Blackberry Falls to guard Chloe, and rightfully so. Grace's fear of others knowing her business and her discomfort with the gossip that went with the small town way of life weren't important right now. Chloe's safety was. Grace would have to withstand the scrutiny that came with others knowing she'd failed to protect her little sister, just as she'd withstood the numerous times her teachers had marched her to her mother's classroom to tell her mother how disobedient she had been.

"Now, what's in the bag?" Evan interrupted her thoughts.

"Chloe's laptop." She pulled the laptop out of the tote sitting beside her feet on the floorboard and settled it on her lap. "I also swiped a couple of hard-copy files from her desk. They were open, so I'm assuming they're files she was working on that kept her at the office so late today. I'll look at those after we get someplace where I can lay everything out. I thought I'd see if I could find clues to help us figure out why someone would want to hurt Chloe."

And me. Opening the screen, she pressed the power button.

"You think her attack is connected to the clinic?"

"I'm not sure. Last week, she discovered drugs missing from the clinic inventory." Grace drummed her fingers on the laptop as she waited for it to boot up.

"What kind of drugs?"

"Clenbuterol and Levothyroxine."

He frowned.

So she explained, "Clenbuterol is a steroid-like drug used to treat breathing disorders in animals, and Levothyroxine is a synthetic T4 hormone replacement used to treat hypothyroidism in both humans and animals."

"Could those drugs be used to make a horse run faster?"

"It's illegal to do so, but yes." Grace typed in the pass code and the computer desktop filled the screen.

"You know your sister's password?"

"It was a guess."

"Obviously a good one. You got it right the first try."

"Chloe doesn't like change, so I tried the password she used for the laptop Dad bought her for her eleventh birthday." Her smile quivered. The memory of Chloe as a child engulfed her. She had thought she was so grown, getting her very own computer. Grace had felt like her father was spoiling his youngest daughter, but he'd insisted the gift was more about providing his girls with a way to stay in touch once Grace left for college than it was giving Chloe free rein on the internet.

That might have been when Chloe's need to video chat when she was in scary situations first developed. She would call Grace at all hours of the night, so she wouldn't feel alone when Dad had been called out to tend to sick animals. Chloe hadn't been left home alone often, but obviously enough for the seeds of dependency to take root.

The screen blurred. She squeezed her eyes tight, fighting the tears burning for release. *Thank you, Lord, for letting me get to Chloe before he could kill her. I'll never complain about her need to video chat again.*

"She'll be okay." Evan's soft baritone filled the silence.

Grace appreciated his attempt to comfort her, but he couldn't know that any more than she did. She concentrated on her breathing as she tried to think of a response.

"I know they sound like empty words. But I mean it. Chloe's a fighter. Always has been."

"Are we talking about the same girl?" What

did he know? When Grace dated him, they'd spent most of their time trying to avoid Chloe with her prying eyes and her constant desire to tag along wherever they went. "Growing up, she never did anything for herself. Always wanting help with her homework and dragging me to the barn to help feed her menagerie of animals."

"That wasn't because she needed help or because she was scared. It was because she loved you and wanted to spend as much time with you as possible. She always knew you'd leave Blackberry Falls."

She sucked in a breath. His words hit like a verbal jab to the heart. His gaze met hers. Breaking contact, she looked down, pretending to focus on the computer screen, tears stinging the backs of her eyes.

Evan cleared his throat. "Other than Chloe's concerns about the clinic, is there anything else going on in her life that might help us determine who's behind the attack?"

"You mean besides her divorce?"

"For the moment, yes."

Ben Hamilton's name came to mind. How did one accuse their father's oldest friend and lifelong neighbor of attempted murder? And for what, a mere eighty acres of land? She rubbed the back of her neck.

"Come on. Out with it. Even if you think it's nothing. We can't afford to overlook any leads."

"Chloe has been receiving letters—offers to buy the farm—from Benjamin Hamilton. He's been getting more persistent lately, even going so far as to tell her why a woman shouldn't live on a farm alone." She sighed. "Looks like he was right. She should have sold to him."

He smiled at her. "Not necessarily. And since we can't change the past, we need to focus on the here and now, which means solving this crime and stopping the attacker from getting to you."

Grace's temples throbbed. *Please don't be a migraine.* She clicked the laptop off, shut the lid and then slipped it into the bag. Leaning back in her seat, she rubbed her tired eyes.

"You didn't find anything useful?"

"I'm not sure what I'm looking for, and my head is starting to hurt." She looked around, trying to figure out where they were. Somewhere along I-25. In the dark, it was hard to tell where exactly. "How much farther?"

"We're almost to the Castle Rock exit. I'd say we're about forty minutes away."

That sounded about right. For the most part, traffic had been light on the drive, but as they got closer to Denver, it would pick up, though 2:00 a.m. traffic wouldn't be anything like the rush hour traffic she'd experienced the evening before. Had it really been less than seven hours since she'd traveled this road in the opposite direction?

"Grace, do you think James could be behind the attack?"

She sat straighter and shifted to look at his profile. "I'm not sure. Before tonight I would have said there was no way. I worried that they'd rushed into marriage. You know, they only dated four months, but from the very beginning, he seemed to dote on her. I first sensed something was wrong at Dad's funeral, but even then, Chloe wouldn't confide in me. It wasn't until…"

He prodded. "Until what?"

Grace had been sworn to secrecy. Did she have the right to share Chloe's secret shame? If James was behind the attack, it could be important to the case. She worried her lower lip.

"Grace. Until what?"

"A year ago, Chloe admitted James had a gambling problem. He'd put them thousands of dollars in debt. She asked me for a loan."

"Did you give it to her?"

"Of course I did. Then a few months ago, right before she filed the divorce paperwork, Chloe confided James had a mistress. Apparently, it wasn't his first."

"Oh, man. It's common knowledge James can be overly friendly to the ladies, but I didn't know he'd cheated on Chloe. Do you know the name of his mistress?"

"I don't remember the name. It was one of the vet techs. Chloe fired her, so she doesn't work at the clinic any longer."

"Marcia O'Neal," Evan stated. "I thought it was odd she took a job at the veterinary hospital in Colorado Springs but continued to live in Blackberry Falls, driving an hour each way to work."

The fact Marcia O'Neal's new job and commute were common knowledge to the chief of police, and most likely ninety percent of the population of Blackberry Falls, didn't shock Grace, but she was thankful at least some of her sister's marital woes had escaped the grapevine.

Hope sparked in her. "If James is behind the attack, why would I be a target? Do you think it was an empty threat to throw us off the trail?"

"Um, I don't think so. For starters, you saw the attacker's face…" He glanced in the rearview mirror and increased his speed. "And it seems we picked up a tail around the Castle Rock exit."

Grace looked out the rear window, the headlights of a vehicle gaining on them temporarily blinding her. Turning back around, she blinked several times to regain focus. "If they've been following us for ten miles, why didn't you try to lose them sooner?"

"I wasn't sure the truck was following us until a couple of miles back. When I sped up and passed those two 18-wheelers, it made every move I did."

"What do we do? We can't lead them to Chloe."

"I don't think getting to Chloe is their priority right now."

"Why do you say that?" She heard the panic in her own voice.

"Because they're making their presence well-known, staying almost bumper-to-bumper."

As if to punctuate his words, the full-size pickup rammed them from behind. Evan jerked the steering wheel to the right and took the exit ramp off the interstate.

The pickup shadowed their every move.

"Grace, get down!"

The authority in his voice had her sliding to the floor as a bullet hit the rear window of their SUV, passed through her headrest and embedded itself in the dashboard.

The threat hadn't been a ruse.

Someone wanted her dead.

Evan had no clue where they were, but estimated Denver city limits was approximately twenty miles away. He hated being in unfamiliar surroundings. His only hope was to lose the vehicle in one of the many suburban neighborhoods and get back on the interstate as soon as possible.

"Are you going to be able to lose him?"

"I'll do my best." The light ahead turned yellow. He gunned the motor. "Hang on." He sped into the intersection—thankful it was the middle of the night and there were no other vehicles around—and, at the last second, turned the wheel sharply to the left, barely missing a light pole. The driver of the truck shot through the intersection.

"Whew. You did it!" Grace's relief exhilarated him, but only momentarily because he knew the driver would maneuver a U-turn and be back on their tail.

"I only bought us a little time. I'm sure he's turning around as we speak." He scanned the area as they sped past a drugstore, gas station and small city park. Did he dare try to find a place to park in the hope the driver wouldn't find them? There didn't seem to be any place to hide, no other vehicles to blend in with. No. Keep moving.

He turned right. Being in unfamiliar surroundings was like being a blindfolded mouse in a maze. He took a left turn and found himself in a neighborhood behind the park.

Evan felt vulnerable. The area was too open. He looked at Grace. Her eyes were closed, her head bowed as if in prayer. She was as innocent as she'd always been. Let her hold to her faith, he'd trust in his own abilities. Flipping the switch on the end of the turn signal lever, he turned off his lights and inched along the sleepy neighborhood street. Headlights swept across the park.

Guided only by the sliver of moonlight, he pulled to the curb and parked in-line with the other cars in front of a row of houses and waited for their pursuer to speed past the park. But the driver didn't speed past. Instead, he turned onto the very street where they waited.

No way to hide a Blackberry Falls police SUV in a Denver suburb. Evan bit back an exclamation, flicked on the lights and raced down the street as fast as he dared.

"He found us." Grace's voice was barely above a whisper.

"Yeah. But don't count me out yet." Evan tried to sound reassuring, but he could hear the doubt in his voice. Why hadn't he changed vehicles? Driving this one was like flashing a neon sign telling the attacker where to find Grace.

He made several turns, barely staying ahead

of the other driver who'd backed off enough to allow himself time to follow Evan's movements. No shots this time. Their pursuer was probably afraid of the prying eyes of a Neighborhood Watch member.

Grace dug into her purse and pulled out her phone. "Shouldn't we call nine-one-one?"

"Only if I can't lose him. In the meantime, use your phone to pinpoint our location. Just in case."

Relaying their exact location would be hard. With his lack of knowledge of the area, Evan couldn't give street names or landmarks to guide the police. His best hope was that an officer cruising the night streets would come upon them speeding through town.

He turned toward what he assumed was the main street and came to an immediate halt. A mechanical railroad-crossing arm blocked his path. The freight engine's light pierced the night, its horn echoing in the silence.

"What are we going to do?" Grace's panicked voice was barely audible above the train's horn.

Their tormentor loomed behind them. They were easy targets for his bullets now. The truck reversed. The hair on the back of Evan's neck prickled. The driver intended to make their deaths look like an accident.

"Hang on to something. He's going to hit

us." Evan engaged the emergency brake and pressed firmly on the floor brake while turning the steering wheel to the right. The SUV jolted, tires squealing and smoke billowing in through the air vents. The breaks held, the impact only moving them a few inches forward. The driver of the truck reversed again. He was building up speed.

Evan released the emergency brake and turned the wheel even more sharply to the right, toward the service road that ran parallel to the tracks. If his plan worked, their attacker might crash, but he and Grace would escape without injury.

"One... Two..." He counted, trying to time their escape. "Three." He jerked the wheel and pressed the gas pedal to the floor when the truck was inches from hitting them. They flew along the service road, and he watched in his rearview mirror as the pickup did a donut spin and come to a stop pointed in the opposite direction. The driver had escaped the collision. It would be a matter of seconds before he started chasing them again. There was only one option.

Picking up speed, Evan raced the train to the next intersection.

"You're going to try to outrun the train!" Horror tainted Grace's accusation. He knew she was thinking about eleventh grade when Tommy

Smithfield tried to cross in front of a train one time too many.

"It's our only option." He didn't dare spare a glance in her direction. "I'll only cut in front of it if I know without a doubt I can make it. I promise." *Please, Lord, help me keep Grace safe.* The prayer came unbidden. Would God answer Evan when he hadn't spoken to Him in so long?

Evan's SUV was neck and neck with the train's engine at the first intersection. He'd have to try the next one. The pursuing lights in his rearview mirror were gaining on them. The next intersection loomed ahead. Warning lights flashed and the mechanical arm started its descent. Evan pressed harder on the gas pedal, shooting forward. *Thank you, Lord.* They would make it.

"Hang on," he ordered Grace for what seemed like the umpteenth time.

Grace's scream mingled with the freight train's horn.

Evan's heart jackhammered against his rib cage as they bounced across the tracks mere seconds ahead of the locomotive. He exhaled. They'd survived. The driver of the truck had been trapped on the other side of the tracks.

Grace was curled into as tight of a ball as possible with her knees pulled to her chest, arms wrapped tightly around them and her head tucked. Her scream turned to sobs. He reached across and touched her arm. "It's okay. We're okay."

Evan's throat tightened as guilt assailed him. If he had changed vehicles, or taken a different route, or something, maybe he could have avoided putting her through this additional trauma. He slid his hand down her arm and laced his fingers with hers, trying to offer calming comfort as his thumb caressed the back of her hand.

He pushed the voice command button on the steering wheel and asked for directions to Denver Memorial that would avoid the interstate.

Several minutes later, Grace's sobs quieted, and she took several deep, concentrated breaths. She pulled her hand free. "I'm sorry. I didn't mean to lose it."

"You've had a traumatic evening."

"Yes, but I should have trusted you. I know you don't take unnecessary chances." She straightened, the seat squeaking with her movement, and peered at the clock on the dashboard: 2:36 a.m. They should have been at the hospital long ago. The cat and mouse game with the man who wanted her and Chloe dead had cost them half an hour.

"How much farther?"

"We should be there in about ten minutes." He nodded toward the map displayed on the screen mounted above the radio. "Sorry, but I thought it best to stay off the interstate. It's less likely our *friend* will find us this way."

"How did you program the map while..." Her words faltered.

Holding her hand?

"Voice command." As if to qualify what he'd said, an animated voice directed him to turn at the next light.

"What if the guy in the truck beats us to the hospital?"

"I think we have a good chance of getting there and out of sight before him. I've been going well above the speed limit to stay ahead of him. Also, with as many hospitals as there are in the Denver metro area, unless he knows exactly which hospital Chloe was taken to, it's likely he'll end up at one of the other ones. No matter what, we'll be on guard."

His cell phone rang, and he pushed the hands-free button on the steering wheel. "Bradshaw here."

"Evan, this is Ryan. You're behind schedule. Is everything okay?"

"We ran into a little trouble. But we're okay. Only a few blocks away. Tell Bridget to watch for us." He disconnected the call.

The automated GPS voice directed him to turn right and take the second left, where they would reach their destination.

He pulled into the ER drop-off area, and Grace unfastened her seat belt, ready to bolt through the doors as soon as he stopped.

"Do not open your door."

"But—"

"Bridget will meet us at the entrance. I'll escort you inside, and she'll park the vehicle."

Letting a civilian drive his police vehicle broke all kinds of rules and regulations, but at this point Evan wasn't ready to trust Grace's safety to anyone other than himself.

FOUR

Every muscle in Grace's body was on high alert, and she desperately wanted to spring out of the vehicle. It had been over three and a half hours since she'd watched the medics put her unresponsive sister into a med-flight helicopter. Much longer and she wouldn't be able to suppress the frustrated scream that clawed at her throat begging for release.

"I need a moment to assess the area and make sure we're safe. Stay seated until I come around." Evan slammed the vehicle into Park and bolted from the driver's seat. He had barely stepped out of the SUV when a petite woman with short, pixie-cut, auburn hair slid into his recently vacated spot.

"Hi, Grace. I don't know if you remember me. Bridget Vincent. Ryan—my brother—is inside guarding Chloe." Bridget prattled on saying something about getting the call from Evan and rushing to the hospital, but Grace couldn't comprehend her words.

She stared at the miniature ball of energy. Bridget had grown into a beautiful woman, but she still talked at warp speed, as if it were some kind of race to see who could get out the most words between breaths.

"Uh…yeah… I remember you," Grace managed to say when Bridget paused.

"We're praying for Chloe. She's a fighter. I'm sure she'll pull through—"

The passenger door opened. "Thanks, Bridget," Evan said as his hand cupped Grace's elbow, helping her out of the SUV. "Don't forget to lock the doors and bring me the keys."

"Sure. No problem. You know I don't mind at—"

Evan closed the door, cutting off Bridget's words, and strode toward the ER entrance, Grace almost sprinting as she struggled to match his pace. "Wasn't trying to be rude, but man, that woman can talk the ears off a donkey."

"That's not nice."

His eyes shone with amusement, and she giggled in spite of herself. Their laughter mingled, echoing off the concrete walls. For a moment, tension lifted from her shoulders and her chest felt less constricted, her breathing lighter. Then guilt assaulted her. How could she laugh with her sister in the hospital fighting for her life?

Evan squeezed her hand and guided her to the security checkpoint. He flashed his badge and explained the situation to the guard. Once they had passes, a nurse escorted them past the main waiting area, through a maze of hallways and into what Grace assumed was the trauma section of the ER.

A man with short black hair, wearing square-framed, black-rimmed glasses, sat in a chair outside Room 13A. Ryan? Bridget had been easily recognizable, but Grace would not have recognized Ryan. It wasn't that his appearance had changed much, but more that he had an air of seriousness and no-nonsense.

How he had gotten permission to stay in this area and guard her sister's door, Grace may never know, but she would be eternally grateful. He stood, shook Evan's hand and then gave her a hug like she was a cousin he hadn't seen in a while.

"I'm sorry this happened." He pulled back and looked her in the eyes, his hands on her shoulders. "But she's in the best place for the best care. We haven't worked out all the details yet, but Bridget and I will help coordinate around-the-clock guard protection until they catch her attacker."

Words failed her, so Grace simply nodded.

A tall, silver-haired, tanned gentleman wearing scrubs and a white lab coat came out of Chloe's room.

"Grace, this is Dr. Carson." Ryan made introductions. "Sir, this is Chloe's sister, Dr. Grace Porter. And Police Chief Evan Bradshaw."

"Dr. Porter."

"DVM not MD." She hurriedly shook the offered hand. "How's my sister? Is she awake?"

"No. Not yet." Dr. Carson moved aside and motioned for her to enter the room ahead of him. "Let's step inside."

She looked to Evan. Would he come with her?

"I need to talk to Ryan. I'll be in soon."

Grace nodded, took a deep breath and went into the room where heart rate monitors and numerous other machines beeped and flashed. Chloe had been intubated, a breathing tube down her throat. She lay perfectly still. Her skin was pasty and there was an ugly bluish-purple bruise on the side of her face. At least she didn't appear to be in distress.

"Is she in pain?" Grace whispered.

"No." Dr. Carson walked over to the monitors and checked the readings before turning back to face her. "We've placed your sister in a medically induced coma. She suffered a brain hemorrhage."

Grace gasped, and he rushed on. "There's a good deal of swelling because of inflammation from the broken vessels, but all scans indicate the bleeding has stopped. Other than that, she has three cracked ribs and a broken wrist. All in all, I'd say Chloe is a very fortunate lady."

"Fortunate? She almost died, and now she's in a coma." The smell of antiseptic mingled with the sharp, stabbing pain behind Grace's left eye, and her vision blurred. This migraine was gearing up to be a doozy. She gripped the bed rail as she fought nausea.

"Medically induced. Once the swelling goes down, we'll wake her up." The doctor touched Grace's arm and searched her face. "Dr. Porter, are you sick?"

"A headache." She puffed out a breath and forced a smile. "I'll be fine. Once I'm sure Chloe's okay. Will she make a full recovery?"

"I can't guarantee anything, but if all goes as planned, then yes."

"And if it doesn't?" Grace questioned, not wanting the answer but needing to know. Bile burning the back of her throat, she rode the wave of pain assailing her.

The doctor hesitated, and she met his gaze. "Please, I need to know."

He gave a nod of agreement. "If the swelling continues, we'll do surgery to relieve the pressure, but she could suffer permanent brain damage."

"And that would mean?"

"At the very least, problems with her fine motor skills and her speech."

Please, Lord, don't let him say it.

"Worst case scenario, she would be in a vegetative state. But I will do everything in my power to keep that from happening." He pulled a chair up closer to the bed, and she sank into it. "Be sure to take something for that headache. I need to go see how much longer it will be until we have a bed for Chloe in the Neuro ICU. You can stay with her until she's moved."

She gasped. "Dr. Carson, the person who attacked my sister is still on the loose. I know ICU staff monitors patients closely, but she can't be unattended at any time."

He squeezed her shoulder. "Don't worry. I'm not sure how he did it, but the young bodyguard out there secured permission from the chief of staff to have a guard stationed outside her room at all times, even in the ICU."

He pulled a peppermint out of his coat pocket and dropped it into her hand. "Maybe this will help until you can eat and take some meds." Dr. Carson gave her a grandfatherly smile and walked out of the room.

Grace scooted closer to Chloe's bed and

wrapped her hand around her sister's cold one. "Oh, Chloe. Please wake up soon and tell us who did this to you. I don't know who I can trust—other than Evan—and I can't keep leaning on him. It would be too easy to fall into old habits, and that wouldn't be good for either of us. He thrives in small town America. You know me, Chloe. Have I ever enjoyed living where I have to wonder who's gossiping about me? Nope." She caressed her sister's hand, wishing she could laugh with her. "You remember the time—"

A creak sounded behind her, and she whirled around. How long had Evan been there? What had he heard?

Evan paced the length of the waiting area and back again. Bits and pieces of Grace's one-sided conversation with Chloe tumbled around in his brain. Why did she always have to see their hometown through such a narrow lens?

His phone vibrated. Lieutenant Johnson's name flashed on the screen.

"Bradshaw here." He spoke in a hushed tone.

"Chief, I wanted to let you know we finished interviewing Dr. James Osborne."

"And?"

"At the time of the attack, he was eating dinner at Aunt Bea's Diner on Highway 9. The owner has been very cooperative and shared the video footage. Osborne arrived at 8:17 p.m. Sat in a booth at the back of the restaurant. Approximately ten minutes later, a brunette in her early-to mid-twenties joined him. She looked familiar, but I've not been able to ID her yet. And Osborne is refusing to give her name."

"Marcia O'Neal."

"Sir?"

"There's a very good chance the woman is a vet tech that the doctor was seeing on the side. Her name is Marcia O'Neal."

"I'll try to verify that information. But, sir, this means his alibi checks out."

"I'm not surprised. Grace saw the attacker's face, so we know it wasn't him. Doesn't mean he isn't behind the attack, though."

"Agreed."

"What do your instincts tell you?" A body language expert, Johnson had an uncanny ability to read people, and Evan trusted his instincts.

"Dr. Osborne seemed genuinely upset about the attack."

"But?"

"I couldn't get a clear sense of his guilt or innocence. He's hiding something. If he's not behind the attack, I suspect he has a good idea who is."

As small as his police force was, Evan didn't

have the manpower to assign officers to watch James Osborne 24/7. He loved being the police chief in a small town, but there were drawbacks, especially when it came to funding. "Okay. Fill the other officers in on what we know so far and make sure they 'unofficially' keep track of the doctor's whereabouts."

"Will do. Anything else?" the lieutenant asked.

"Hold down the fort until I get back."

"When will that be?"

A soft snore pulled his attention back to the room.

Grace had fallen asleep, twisted sideways in a lime-green, vinyl chair, her legs draped across the arm and her head tilted awkwardly against the wall. He knew exhaustion had claimed her soon after her sister had been moved to a room in Neuro ICU. Earlier, she'd downed two pain pills and guzzled a vending machine coffee. He hoped her headache was gone when she woke but was afraid it would be replaced with a crick in her neck. Sitting beside Grace, Bridget flipped through a magazine, lifting her gaze to the door every few seconds, always on alert.

"Chief? Are you still there?" Johnson's voice sounded in his ear.

"Yeah. My goal is to be back by three so I can pick Camden up from school." He looked out the bank of windows on the east-facing wall of the waiting room. The sun had risen, and traffic was increasing. The morning rush hour would soon be in full swing. "I still need to finalize a plan to provide around-the-clock guards for Chloe."

"About that. The patrol officers and I have decided we'll take care of guard duty."

"I wish it were that easy." Evan sighed. "Not only can I not afford to pay overtime for you guys to serve as guards, but it's over a two-hour drive, one-way."

"No, you don't understand. We're volunteering our time on our days off."

"What? Are you serious? I can't ask you to do that."

"You're not asking."

"But—"

"No, sir." Johnson cut him off. "We've made our minds up. Chloe Osborne is one of our own. Most of us have known her since grade school. A few of us even took her out a time or two in high school, myself included. Blackberry Falls is about community and family. We take care of both."

Can't argue with his logic.

To be honest, Evan was relieved he wouldn't have to approach the Denver chief to ask for assistance. They'd had words the night Lisa had been killed in a drive-by shooting a block from the hotel where they were staying. Granted,

Evan bore most of the responsibility for agreeing to walk back to the hotel following the play instead of insisting on taking a cab. He had known the streets could be dangerous at that time of night, but Lisa had wanted to enjoy the evening a little longer. The hotel had been less than two blocks away, and she could be very persuasive when she wanted to be. He'd been happy to see her smile again.

"All right, then. Text me a schedule of the rotation. I'll pass it along to Ryan, so he can notify the hospital staff. He and Bridget will also fill in any gaps in the schedule as needed. Oh—and, Johnson, make sure the officers know if their relief is late arriving, they are not to leave their post, even if it means they're late for work. We'll cover for them, and their pay won't be docked."

"Yes, sir."

Disconnecting the call, Evan slipped the phone into his pocket. An elderly man with a walker entered the waiting area, followed by a blue-haired woman of similar age and a dark-haired girl who looked to be in her early twenties. The hospital buzzed with morning activity. As much as he'd like to let Grace sleep a little longer, he needed to wake her and find a more private area for them to discuss a plan to keep her safe after he headed home.

Home. Growing up moving from one military base to the other, Blackberry Falls had felt like home from the moment his family had settled there following his father's retirement from the Air Force. The moment he'd first seen the town—its Main Street decorated with American flags for Memorial Day, the large park at the center of the town square, and the endless hiking trails into the Rocky Mountains with one leading to the waterfall the town had been named for—he had known he never wanted to leave.

Just one of the reasons he would never understand why Grace had been in such a hurry to leave the only home she'd ever known.

Grace's migraine had lessened, but her senses remained on hyper alert—even the roots of her hair ached. She rubbed her temples and tried to focus on Evan's words.

"I've worked everything out. You can be in the comfort of your own home and be here for your sister. Bridget will stay with you at night and bring you back to the hospital each morning."

He wanted her to stay in Denver? She had felt certain he'd insist on her returning to Blackberry Falls where he could keep an eye on her.

"One of my off-duty officers will be here, stationed right outside Chloe's door." Evan looked at her, then continued in a rush. "You'll have to stay in Chloe's room, only stepping out and staying with the guard when the doctors or nurses ask you to. At the end of the day, Ryan or Bridget will pick you up and escort you home. No venturing out, because I won't have a guard who can go with you. Do you understand?"

Relief flooded through her. She'd stay by her sister's bedside and watch over her, ensuring her safety. Then a niggle of doubt worked its way into her brain. The doctors and nurses were the people her sister needed to take care of her, not Grace. They were the ones who could make her comfortable. And the off-duty police officers who—for whatever reason she could not imagine—were volunteering time away from their own families, were the ones who could protect her. There wasn't much Grace could do here.

She bit her lower lip. Staying at the hospital would be selfish. Grace would be hiding out. She'd be a bigger help to her sister if she went back to Blackberry Falls, took care of the clinic and looked for clues as to who wanted them both dead. "No. I mean yes, I understand. No, I won't stay here."

"Don't be stubborn, Gracie." Evan dragged a hand over his face where stubble had transformed his normally clean-cut, guy-next-door look into one of a rugged outdoorsman. "I knew you wouldn't enjoy having to stay in one place all day, but it's the best I can do."

"It's not that. I need to take care of things at the clinic."

If she couldn't make him understand, he'd insist she stay here, under lock and key. "James is scheduled to leave at the end of next week, after they finalize the divorce. In the meantime, I need him to go over the patient files with me and fill me in on the ins and outs of his caseload. I also need to start interviewing for a new vet. Besides, I also have Barkley to consider. He'll be sad his owner is missing and will need extra attention."

"Be reasonable." His voice boomed in the small walk-in-closet-size room where they waited to talk with Dr. Carson and receive an update on Chloe. Lowering his voice, Evan added, "I don't have the manpower to protect you at the clinic."

"I'll be fine at the clinic. I won't be alone. There are always a lot of people around."

"What about after work? Who will guard you then? Am I going to have to spend the nights in my car outside the farmhouse waiting for the man to come back to try to kill you?"

"No. You have a child who needs you at home. Look. I know you'd prefer to keep me under twenty-four-hour security, miles away from Blackberry Falls, but do you think that will stop someone who wants me dead?"

He paled, as if she'd slapped him. She'd heard he'd been walking right beside his wife when she was shot and hadn't been able to stop it from happening. Knowing him as well as she did, she knew he blamed himself. He needn't worry. Grace had lived on her own for almost half her life. She knew how to be cautious and wouldn't take unnecessary risks.

"I'll stay in the apartment above the clinic. It's only a few miles from the police station, and I'll set the alarm system the second the last employee leaves."

"What if the last employee to leave is James? We've not ruled him out as a suspect yet."

"I'll make sure he isn't the last one."

"How can you guarantee that?"

"I'll come up with some excuse for him to leave early, an errand or something. If that fails, I'll leave with the other employees. I'm sure Valerie would be happy to drive me to the police station."

Valerie had been an employee at the clinic longer than anyone else, starting as a part-time employee in high school and later becoming a veterinary technician. She had become a close family friend. Grace knew she'd do as asked without question.

"Once you get off work, you can take me

back to the clinic, check everything out, and make sure things are locked up tight."

Evan still looked doubtful, so she added, "I promise to be careful, but if these attacks are connected to whatever Chloe discovered at the clinic, you'll need someone on the inside looking for clues."

"I think you've been watching too many whodunit movies."

"No, but I enjoy true crime shows. Do you have enough info to secure a search warrant at the clinic?"

"No. However, as co-owner, you can give us permission without a warrant."

"I can give you access to general information, like billing and drug supplies, not patient records. That would be unethical. If you found something in the records I gave you access to, James would probably be long gone before you could secure a search warrant for his files. Admit it, you need my help."

He shoved his hand through his hair. "If I go along with this, you must promise not to take any risks. I have to know your whereabouts at all times."

She'd never liked having her every move analyzed, but if that's what it took to get him to let her go back to help look for the person wanting her and Chloe dead, then so be it.

FIVE

Evan was late. He turned onto the road that circled around to the back of Blackberry Falls Elementary School and pulled into the car-rider pickup line, nodding a return greeting to parents who waved as they drove past. There were a dozen or so cars ahead of him in line. Hopefully, Camden hadn't become apprehensive. The anxiety attacks had started the second month of kindergarten, when Evan had been late because he'd stopped to offer aid to a stranded motorist. The counselor had told him the attacks were a result of Camden's fear of something happening to his only living parent.

Camden had only been twenty months old when Lisa died, too young to have many memories of her. When he'd started school and had realized most of his classmates had two parents, he'd started crying himself to sleep at night and didn't want to let Evan out of his sight.

The car in front of them pulled forward, and

he followed. Only five cars ahead of him now, he was close enough to see the children waiting on the sidewalk, their backs against the building. Camden stood next to the assistant principal, Ms. Sims, his gaze downcast and shoulders slouched.

His son's pain ripped at Evan's heart, which was why he'd do anything within his power to eliminate his fears, including dragging Grace to the school. "I'm sorry I wasn't able to drop you off at the clinic first. It's important for me to pick Camden up on time."

She nodded. "It's fine."

"Lisa's mom normally picks Cam up, but she and her husband had to fly to Arizona for the birth of a grandchild. They'll be gone for two weeks." Which was why Cam had spent the night with them last night, a school night, and why Evan had been the one to respond to Grace's 9-1-1 call.

"It's okay, I understand."

"Thank you. Did you get a chance to talk to Valerie?" He still wasn't convinced Grace's plan was a good one. However, he also couldn't guarantee any of the clinic employees were safe, with or without her presence. For the time being, he'd increase the patrols in the area, and he'd make a point of either him or another officer being at the clinic before the end of day. They could help her lock up and secure the premises.

"No. Other than a text early this morning asking her to take care of Barkley until I got back. I can fill her in once we get to the clinic."

"Don't tell her too much. The fewer people who know we suspect a connection to the clinic, the better."

"Don't worry. I'm not one who overshares."

Evan remembered. Like she hadn't shared her intentions of going away to school and never returning.

He pulled forward. Ms. Sims said something to Camden, and he looked up and spotted the police vehicle, relief flooding his little face. Evan waved.

The car in front of them pulled away from the curb, and he slid into the vacated spot, rolling down the window. "Sorry I'm late."

"It's okay, Dad." The words sounded good, but the smile looked forced. Poor guy. Evan had called his mom earlier to see if she could pick Camden up, but she'd been at a dentist's appointment. There were less than two weeks left in the school year, but next year, Evan would need a better backup plan for someone to pick up Camden from school in an emergency.

"You're not late at all, chief." The administrator opened the back door, and Camden climbed into the booster seat Evan had hurriedly picked up at a big-box store on their return from Denver. "See you, Monday, Camden." Mrs. Sims shut the door and waved Evan on, ensuring the car-rider line ran like a well-oiled machine.

He pulled up to the stop sign and glanced in his rearview mirror. "Hey, sport. Did you have a good day?" Camden didn't reply. His gaze was fixed on Grace. "Camden, this is Dr. Porter. She's a veterinarian. We're giving her a ride to Porter Animal Clinic."

The smile that split Cam's face was genuine and reached all the way to the green eyes he'd inherited from his mother. "Oh, boy! Can I pet the animals?"

"It's not a zoo—"

"You can't pet the patients," Grace interrupted, twisting in her seat to smile at Camden. "But I'm sure Barkley would love some attention."

"Gracie, I'm—"

"Who's Barkley?" Camden asked.

"My sister's dog. I'm dog-sitting him for a while."

"Is he a puppy?"

She giggled. "No, he's a full-grown dog."

"Full-grown pony," Evan muttered under his breath. In his peripheral vision, he saw Grace's smile widen. She'd heard him.

A horn blared behind them. Great. He'd stalled the movement of the car-rider line. He pulled out of the parking lot and headed north, half listening to the conversation between Grace and his son.

"How old is Barkley?"

"He's three."

"Three?" Shock laced Camden's little voice. "He's a baby. I'm six. I'm more grown than him," he added emphatically.

Don't rush it son. Don't rush it.

A melodious laugh emanated from Grace. "I don't think anyone can call Barkley a baby. Wait until you meet him. He's bigger than you are."

"No way," Camden protested. Then he started telling Grace all the things he was taller than.

A grin tugged at Evan's lips. When he'd seen Camden's crestfallen face, he'd been sure it would be a long, quiet ride home, but somehow Grace had turned it around.

Ten minutes later, he pulled the SUV into the parking lot of the Porter Animal Clinic. The lot was empty, except for the two vehicles in the employee parking area at the side of the building. One was James Osborne's luxury sports car, but Evan wasn't sure who owned the other, less pretentious, economy vehicle.

"Looks like business is slow today," he said, parking in the spot closest to the front door.

"What? That doesn't make sense. I imagined the place would be swamped with nosy busy-bodies wanting to get the latest gossip."

"Grace, the people in this town care about your sister. If they're talking about her, it's not to gossip. It's because they're worried."

"Wait. There's a sign on the door," Grace noted, ignoring his words. She leaned forward. "'Temporarily closed because of a family emergency.'"

She unfastened her seat belt and opened her door. "What are they thinking?"

"Hold on." Evan bolted out of his seat and rushed around the back of the vehicle, scanning the area. Nothing seemed out of place.

"Don't forget me, Dad." Camden banged his hand on the window, child security locks preventing him from letting himself out. Evan mentally kicked himself. Why hadn't he found a babysitter for Cam? Because he hadn't known whom to call, since he'd never needed a sitter before with both his and Lisa's parents living close by and happy to help.

Grace had already barged through the door of the clinic. He had to follow her. What about Camden? Would he be safer in the vehicle? The temperatures were still cool, but Evan couldn't take a chance. Nothing to do but let Camden out of the backseat and follow her.

"Son, I need you to obey me at all times while we're here. Do you understand?"

"Yes, sir."

"I mean it, Cam. Don't wander off. Stay where I tell you and listen to all my commands."

"Got it. Now can I see Barkley?"

He escorted his small son into what should have been a fun and exciting environment, but for today was scary and unknown.

Lord, I pray I'm not putting Cam in danger.

Two prayers in one day. Could he be learning to talk to the Lord again?

The twenty-third Psalm instantly sprang to mind.

Grace seethed. What had James been thinking? Why had he closed the clinic today? Dad had never closed the clinic during regular business hours. If he'd been unable to work, the office staff, vet techs and veterinary assistants still reported to the clinic to handle nonmedical emergency issues and to redirect emergencies to a veterinarian in a nearby town.

The waiting area was empty. She glanced in the exam rooms, also empty. Next was James's private office. Again empty. Where was he? She'd seen his vehicle. She knew he was there. The sound of drawers slamming came from her sister's office.

She rounded the receptionist's desk. "James? Why is the clinic closed?"

He strolled out of Chloe's office. "Because I didn't want to spend the day answering questions about why I was here and not at the hospital with Chloe."

"If you didn't want people gossiping about your marital affairs, you should have been faithful to your wife."

James startled, and his eyes widened.

"Yes. Chloe told me. What I'm more interested in right now is what you were doing in her office."

"I don't owe you an explanation." He pushed past her, headed for the front door.

"Actually, you do."

He pivoted on his heel and glared at her. "Do what?"

"Owe me an explanation." She met his eyes and willed her voice to remain steady, while her insides rattled as if an 8.0 quake had shaken the earth. Maybe it was having her life threatened twice in a matter of hours. Maybe it was because she'd failed Chloe as a big sister and she needed to make it right. Normally, Grace hated conflict, but she needed answers. "In case you've forgotten because of my absence, I'm co-owner of the clinic. So that makes me your boss."

He leaned in close. "What are you going to do, fire me? Chloe's lawyer took care of that when he served me with papers. Didn't he? That's why you're here, after all. Well, it's all yours. If you can hold on to it, that is."

The bell over the front door jingled and Evan entered, a firm grasp on Camden's hand.

"Where are the puppy dogs?" Camden struggled to pull free of his dad's grip, but Evan held firm. "Dr. Porter said I could meet Barkley."

"In a minute, son." He escorted the child across the waiting area and stood beside her, his gaze fixed on James. "After Dr. Porter finishes talking to Dr. Osborne."

"We're finished. Dr. Porter was just showing me the door," James scoffed. "Good luck finding someone to replace me." He turned and strode out of the building.

"What was that all about?"

"I'm not sure. He was in Chloe's office. I think he was searching for something." She inhaled sharply. "The tote bag is still in your car. Do you think he was looking for her computer?"

"I don't know." Evan knelt to eye level with his son, the child a miniature version of his father, save for the green eyes. "Stay with Dr. Porter while I get her bag out of the car."

Grace desperately wanted to rush into her sister's office and start searching through files, but she couldn't very well do that with a child in tow. "So, how about we go find Barkley, and then you can help me feed him?"

"Oh, boy!" Camden put his small hand into hers. "I begged Dad for a puppy, but he said I'm not old enough. Dr. Porter, how old do ya have to be to get a pet? My dad's really old! Shouldn't he be old enough to have one? If it was his pet, I could still play with it." The child rattled on while they walked, not pausing long enough for her to respond.

Grace led him toward the rear door. Hopefully, Valerie had put Barkley in the fenced-in kennel area instead of leaving him in the apartment all day. She reached for the knob, but the door opened before she could touch it. She gasped and shoved Camden behind her, blocking him from danger.

"Grace!"

"Oh!" She pressed a hand against her chest, as if the pressure could slow down the hammering of her heart. "Valerie, you startled me."

The tall, slender, black-haired woman who looked like she should be on a runway in New York City stepped across the threshold, Barkley at her heels. "I'm sorry. I was feeding the animals when I saw the chief's SUV pull in. I thought you might be here to pick up Barkley."

The massive Great Dane almost knocked

Grace down as he scrambled to check out the little boy peeking from behind her legs. "Camden, this is Barkley."

"He's a giant!" The child stared in awe.

"A gentle giant." She laughed. "Barkley, sit."

The animal obeyed, his tail tapping a steady beat against the concrete floor. Grace knelt and ran her hands through his soft fur, rubbing the back of his neck. "It's okay to pet him. Gently rub your hand over his shoulder. Good."

Barkley licked Camden's face, and the child giggled. "He likes me."

"Of course he does." She stood and faced Valerie. "Thank you for taking care of him today."

"No problem." The veterinarian technician's face grew solemn. "How's Chloe? I heard you saved her—and you saw the attacker's face." Valerie moved in closer and added in a hushed tone, "Can you identify him?"

A shiver went up Grace's arm. How did Valerie know she'd seen the attacker's face? Grace had only told Evan, and he wouldn't have told anyone other than on a need-to-know basis. Her throat constricted. She shook her head and stepped back.

Valerie offered her a sympathetic smile. "I couldn't believe something like that could happen in our small town. Everyone's on edge, wondering if this person will attack again. My mom is even locking her doors in the daytime. Why, I stopped by for lunch today and had to ring the doorbell."

An internal struggle, so familiar in her childhood, started in the pit of Grace's stomach. Be honest with her lifelong friend and admit her fears Chloe wouldn't survive and risk everything she said being front-page news tomorrow, or act as if everything was fine?

"There's no evidence the citizens of Blackberry Falls are in danger." Evan stepped into the hallway and ruffled his son's hair, a smile lighting his face. "But it's always a good idea to keep your doors locked, even in a small town."

Gratitude washed over Grace. Once again, Evan had saved her. He'd done that numerous times in the last nineteen hours. First, protecting her from the person who wanted her dead, and now saving her from answering a difficult question. After fifteen years of being independent and on her own, Grace was afraid she was getting used to him being there for her. And that terrified her.

Grace opened one eye and looked at the clock on the bedside table. Three seventeen. Living alone had never spooked her, and the mental and physical exhaustion of the previous twenty-four hours had given her the hope of a sound night's sleep. Instead, she'd heard every creak and rumble of the night—cars, animals and unidentified thuds and bumps. It had been after midnight before she had closed her eyes, only to awaken every twenty minutes or so. In total, she'd probably slept less than an hour.

She flopped onto her back and stared at the ceiling.

Evan had called a locksmith to change all the locks and codes on every exterior door in the clinic and the apartment. Then he'd insisted on staying with her until Camden's bedtime. He ordered a pizza and chocolate-chip cookies from a local restaurant. After dinner, Camden and Barkley played together on the floor while she and Evan sat on the couch viewing the files on Chloe's computer. To an observer, she was sure the scene would have looked like a typical family evening. That is until Evan checked all the doors, both in the clinic and the apartment, to ensure they were locked, did a full perimeter check, ordered hourly police patrols and drove off into the night with his son, while she and Barkley watched from the window.

Throwing the cover off, Grace got out of bed and plodded into the kitchen for a drink of water. Her mind replayed the events of the day. Why had James been so evasive when Grace had asked what he'd been doing in Chloe's office? He had to have been searching for something. But what?

Her eyes fell upon the tote lying on the small kitchen table, the computer sitting off to the side. She picked up the bag and peered inside. She'd completely forgotten about the file folders. Grace had looked over them briefly at the hospital, but nothing had seemed out of place. What was she missing?

Pulling the files out of the bag, she laid them open. Typical billing records. Dates and types of service, insurance payment, if any, and account balances.

Wait a minute.

She picked up the last folder she had slipped into the bag, the one that had been half hidden under the desk blotter. These weren't accounting records, they were medical records.

Why would Chloe—who had a master's in business administration and worked as the office manager—have medical records hidden in her office? And why a printed copy? The clinic used an online database to store and streamline patient records. They didn't keep hard-copy files any longer.

She scanned the pages. A toxicology report and a necropsy report. The patient, a three-year-old Thoroughbred stallion named Mountain Shadow, had died of sudden heart failure.

At the time of death, in addition to high doses of caffeine, he also had high levels of Clenbuterol and Levothyroxine in his system. The two drugs Chloe had said were missing from inventory.

Grace powered up the computer, then turned and searched the cabinets for coffee pods. She needed something stronger than water since it looked like she wouldn't be going back to bed anytime soon.

Steaming mug in hand, she scooped the laptop off the table and made her way to the faded green-plaid sofa in the small sitting area. Placing the mug on the side table, she sat and tucked one foot under her.

Barkley plodded out of the bedroom and lay on the floor in front of the sofa.

"You miss Chloe, don't you, buddy?" Grace leaned over and scratched the Great Dane's head, and he licked her palm. "It's going to be okay. She'll be back soon, and you'll get all kinds of loving."

The dog yawned and laid his head down.

"Good boy. You get some rest while I work."

She clicked the icon to access the online database and typed in the password.

Please, Lord, let my hunch be wrong.

She clicked on the search box and typed Mountain Shadow. After the spinning circle stopped, she opened the medical history and read the toxicology report. All the drugs listed on the paper copy were listed in the electronic file, but someone had lowered the toxicity levels. A careless typo by the transcriptionist? She didn't think so.

Next, she opened the electronic copy of the necropsy report. Cause of death was listed as heart failure due to a ventricular septal defect. A hole in the heart. A defect the Thoroughbred would have been born with. Why would someone falsify the clinic's records? No, not why. Why was obvious. The stallion had died from an overdose of metabolism-enhancing drugs. Someone wanted to cover up the cause of death. The real question was who. The transcriptionist? One of the vet techs? James?

Barkley got up, went to the door, whimpered and then looked back at her.

"Do you need to go out, boy? Hmm?" Closing the laptop, Grace stood and stretched before crossing to the door. She patted Barkley's back and then reached for the handle. And paused, her hand on the knob. Evan had only allowed her to stay at the apartment if she agreed to remain inside with the doors locked at all times.

She looked out the window. The faintest hint of morning light had started to peek in the distance, but it would be another thirty minutes or longer before the sun rose.

The Great Dane whimpered and scratched at the door.

The clinic didn't open until seven, and the staff wouldn't arrive until a quarter till. Barkley could not wait hours to relieve himself. She sighed.

Though technically outside, the kennel was a fully enclosed, locked area accessed via a door from the main building. There was a small grassy area, so the Great Dane could do his business.

"Barkley, come." She snagged her cell phone off the coffee table and slipped it into her pocket.

Opening the door that led downstairs into the clinic, she allowed Barkley to take the lead, their steps guided only by the night-lights spaced randomly along the hallway. Her heart picked up tempo with every step she took, as if she were an intruder afraid of being caught. Pressing a hand against her chest, she puffed out a breath of air.

Grace wouldn't really be breaking her promise to Evan. She'd stay inside the doorway and wouldn't step outside. No one would see her.

"Okay, boy. Go." She opened the door and the Great Dane darted out into the kennel. Some of the boarded animals stirred and barked a greeting. Others lay undisturbed. Barkley went from cage to cage, sniffing the area.

"Hurry, boy. Do your business and let's get back upstairs."

Barkley ambled over to the grass then headed back in her direction, until something outside the fence caught his attention. He stood tall and regal, his ears straight up and his tail back, a low growl emanating from deep in his throat. The growl grew into a fierce bark, causing the hair on the nape of her neck to stand and goose bumps to pop up along her arms.

What had the animal seen? Did she dare go look? No, she'd watched enough horror movies to know that wouldn't end well. *Get back upstairs to safety and call the police.* That's what she would be yelling to the heroine on the television screen in this scenario.

She whistled softly. "Barkley, in."

The animal disregarded the command, his growling bark becoming more aggressive. She needed to get upstairs but didn't want to leave her sister's beloved pet behind.

Ignoring the internal voice silently screaming, *Don't do it*, she inched one foot in front of the other and took a few steps into the kennel, staying behind the cages.

Heavy footsteps crunched on the gravel outside the fence. Slipping her phone out of her pocket, she pressed speed dial, thankful Evan had programmed the important numbers into her phone before leaving last night.

"Come on, answer the phone." Grace bounced nervously from foot to foot as she counted the rings. *Two...three...*"Bark—"

"Blackberry Falls Police Department." An authoritative female voice sounded across the line.

"I'm at Porter Animal Clinic." Grace spoke barely above a whisper. "I need an officer. There's someone outside."

"Is this Dr. Porter?"

"Yes."

"Where are you in the building?"

"We're in the kennel."

"We? Who's with you?"

"My sister's dog."

"Find somewhere to hide and stay on the line. An officer is on the way."

The metal chain-link fence rattled. Was the person trying to climb into the kennel?

Grace's breath caught in her throat. She stumbled and clutched the bars of the cage closest to her. This drew Barkley's attention. He headed toward her and then stopped, turned and growled again.

Peering around the cage, she spotted a shadowy figure straddling the six-foot fence. He threw his leg over and dropped into the kennel.

"Barkley, come!" She turned and raced indoors.

For all his barking and growling, the Great Dane was as scared as Grace and stayed at her heels entering the building.

She slammed the door shut and locked it.

"The intruder's inside the fence!" She yelled into the phone. "Tell the officer to hurry."

The shadow man loomed on the other side of the frosted-glass door. The doorknob rattled. Barkley whimpered and headed for the apartment. Grace backed away, then turned and ran after Barkley.

"Dr. Porter. What's happening?"

The door busted open.

"He's inside." Her words came out in a husky whisper.

Her phone beeped and went silent. Dead battery. Grace slid the phone into her back pocket. And ran. Four more steps to the top of the stairs and her apartment.

He gained on her. Now, only a few steps below her.

Half turning, she grasped the rail, raised her leg and kicked as hard as she could. Her foot connected with his chest. The man stumbled and fell backward with a heavy thud.

He lay unmoving at the foot of the stairs, arms and legs spread-eagle, a ski mask hiding his identity. She itched to remove it to see his face, but she didn't dare get near him. What if he was only winded and not unconscious? As if to answer her unspoken question, the man groaned and started to push to his knees.

Grace turned and darted the rest of the way up the stairs. *Lord, please let help arrive in time.*

SIX

A ringing phone shattered the early morning quiet. Evan woke with a start and pushed himself up into a seated position. Snatching his cell off the nightstand, he checked the screen. Blackberry Falls PD.

He was on instant alert. "Bradshaw here."

"Chief. There was an intruder at Porter Animal Clinic." Reba Franklin, the night shift dispatcher, had his full attention.

"Is Grace okay?" Jumping out of bed, he put the phone on speaker, tossed it onto the bedside table and hurriedly pulled on a pair of jeans and a T-shirt.

"We think so, sir."

"What do you mean you think so?" Why was his dispatcher talking in circles? "Tell me what you know."

"Dr. Porter called the station approximately ten minutes ago. Someone was outside the kennel. They made entry. At that time, we lost communication with Dr. Porter."

Fear gripped him. Why had he left her there alone?

The dispatcher continued. "When Officer Wilkes arrived at the clinic, the side door was ajar. He entered the building. There were signs of a break-in and a struggle, but the intruder had fled the scene. Dr. Porter had barricaded herself in the apartment. She's shaken up and insists on giving her statement to you."

"Is Wilkes with her now?"

"Yes, sir."

"Tell him to stay with her. I'm on my way." Disconnecting, he tried Grace's cell, but the call went straight to voice mail. He shoved his feet into a pair of running shoes and bent to tie them. Then he grabbed his wallet and keys off the dresser before crossing to the nightstand and retrieving his service revolver from the locked box. Time to roll.

He walked into the hallway and froze. Camden. He'd call his mom from the car and let her know he needed to drop him off at her house.

Evan entered the small room decorated in a superhero theme. His path illuminated by a Spider-Man night-light, he stepped around the toy cars and plastic dinosaurs littering the floor.

Bending, he grabbed a pair of tennis shoes

off the floor then scooped his still-sleeping, pajama-clad son up into his arms and headed for the garage.

"Where are we going?" Camden mumbled, his eyes still closed as Evan put him in the SUV.

"Grammy's house," Evan answered as he secured the seat belt across the booster seat.

His son's green eyes opened and peered at him accusingly. "You promised we'd go fishing today."

Evan groaned inwardly. He *had* promised, after missing the end of the school year picnic. Thankfully, school would be out for summer break soon, giving him one less thing to juggle.

"The day has just started." He ruffled Camden's hair, then climbed into the driver's seat and backed out of the garage. "First, you get to hang out with Grammy and Poppy, have breakfast and watch cartoons. Then, when I get back, we'll go fishing."

You, me, Grace and Barkley. If she's okay. Please, let her be okay.

He desperately wanted to turn on the lights and sirens as he raced to her, but he didn't want to frighten Cam.

By the time they arrived at his parents' house, his son was wide-awake. His mother met them in the driveway, wearing her nightgown and housecoat. She opened the back door and unbuckled Camden, who, once free, raced into the house.

Libby Bradshaw poked her head through Evan's open window. "Don't worry about a thing, son. Cam's fine here as long as necessary. You take care of Grace and concentrate on finding the person trying to hurt her and her sister."

"Yes, ma'am." Having grown up in a military family, he always used "ma'am" and "sir" when talking to his parents. "And thanks, Mom."

She kissed his cheek and hurried indoors.

He may never have a wife and Camden may never have a mother in his life again, but they had his parents and Lisa's parents. Evan had spent too long feeling sorry for himself and focusing on past mistakes, maybe it was time he started counting his blessings instead of his failures.

Backing out of the drive, Evan flipped on the siren and sped toward Porter Animal Clinic and Grace.

He pulled into a parking spot beside the other patrol car and raced up the outside stairs that led to the apartment, ignoring the neighbors and community members gathering in clusters on porches and outside other businesses. It was natural for people to be curious and concerned when a police cruiser, or two, showed up out-